THE TERROR OF TIBA

Titles in this series

MISSING!
FIRST PONY
SECRET OF ZARB
SOUND OF DANGER
DUEL IN THE SNOW
PADDY TURNS DETECTIVE
THE EAGLE AND THE HAWK
THE PENHALLOW MYSTERY
JACKY JUMPS TO THE TOP
SECRET OF THE SHADOW
GUN TRAIL TO SEDALIA
THE IDOL OF EL ABRA
THE MENACE OF MASK
PERILOUS ADVENTURE
STRANGERS IN SPACE
LAST OUT OF BURMA
DANGER AT DARREL
SUBMARINE KILLER
DOOMED TRAWLER
PONY CLUB CAMP
TERROR OF TIBA
AFRAID TO RIDE
TENDERFOOT
COMMANDO

BASIL DEAKIN

THE TERROR OF TIBA

Collins
LONDON AND GLASGOW

First published 1967

PRINTED AND MADE IN GREAT BRITAIN BY
WM. COLLINS SONS AND CO. LTD.
LONDON AND GLASGOW

Chapter One

"UP PERISCOPE!"

Rod Renton, top security agent to Britain's secret Missile Defence Service, watched with tense interest the thick stem of the periscope quietly rising in its casing. At Rod's side, Mat Malloy, his assistant, waited keenly for the submarine commander's next order.

"Steady as she goes. Motors at half-speed. Ah! Excellent! Take a look for yourself, Renton."

Rod stepped up to the periscope and peered intently at the dark scene on the surface above them.

"All looks quiet," he remarked as he stepped aside to let Mat stare into the reflected image through the periscope sights. "Water looks calm. I can see breakers on the beach, but I reckon we can make it in a rubber dinghy."

Mat was staring towards the beach of the night-shrouded island dead ahead of the almost motionless submarine. Silhouetted against the dark sky, tall palm trees waved lazily in the night breeze. The distant beach lay black and empty as far as he could see; but away to the right, at the far end of the island, lights glowed.

"That will be the British air base on the Pacific island of Tiba," Rod commented when Mat remarked on the lights. "The base is divided from the rest of Tiba by a boundary line."

"Sure," Mat nodded. "I wonder what's going on over there and why, without explanation, Barada, the ruler of Tiba, has closed the boundary, forbidden the British to cross it and ordered us out of Tiba?"

The submarine commander eyed them both grimly.

"Is that why you two are making a midnight landing on Tiba?" he questioned. "To discover why Barada is trying to break his treaty with Britain?"

"As you must have guessed, our mission is top secret," Rod replied, his tone stern. "But what you say is just about the size of it, Commander. Barada has always been a good ally to Britain. Suddenly, he has become anti-British, ordered our air base to close down and we've to get out of Tiba."

"Phew!" the commander blew out his cheeks in consternation. "The base is vital for Britain's Far East defence plans. Without it, we'd be in a very serious position strategically. What do you two reckon on doing?"

"Find out what is behind Barada's sudden change of mind," Rod snapped tersely. "We've got to discover why he is trying to break his treaty with Britain, *and prevent him doing so.* The terrible danger for Britain is that the East Power will move in and seize the air base if Barada succeeds in driving us out of Tiba."

"Stand by to surface!"

The commander's order rang through the vessel. In response to the order the submarine's motors rose in pitch as the ballast tanks began to blow. With a barely perceptible movement the submarine ascended until, through its steel hull, water could be heard cascading off the rising decks.

At once, all was orderly bustle. Forward, the deck hatch was raised and sailors clambered on to the wet decking with an inflatable rubber dinghy, while Rod and Mat followed the commander up the steel ladder of the conning tower to the bridge.

Once on the bridge, Rod stared long and searchingly through the commander's powerful night binoculars, his gaze sweeping slowly along the sandy shore a mile or so distant.

"Looks quiet and deserted," he stated at last. "A hundred yards or so of beach, then palm trees and jungle. If the dinghy is inflated, Commander, we'll be on our way. Down to the deck, Mat!"

No time was wasted in slithering the dinghy down the shell of the submarine on to the water. Rod and Mat leaped aboard and with a brief wave, pushed off.

"Keep as low as you can," Rod ordered. "The less silhouette we make against the skyline the better—just in case there are any probing eyes hidden among those palm trees at the back of the beach."

Mat grinned. "Do you figure we might get a warm reception if we are spotted?"

"What do you think?" Rod retorted. "A boat sneaking in under cover of the dark, at midnight! That isn't exactly what any self-respecting tripper would be doing, is it? Don't forget Barada has closed Tiba to all outsiders. So you can figure we wouldn't get a 'welcome-on-the-mat' reception if we were sighted."

Silently, and warily watching the beach while they paddled towards it, Rod and Mat urged their rubber dinghy towards the darkened shore line.

"Look!" Mat whispered, stabbing the dark with his forefinger.

Rod's gaze flashed in the direction of Mat's outstretched arm. He saw nothing but the shadowy outlines of the gently swaying palm trees towering above the jungle.

"What is it?" he hissed.

"A light," Mat muttered. "Flashed on and then vanished. Somewhere among those palms."

Their craft dived into a trough, and the beach was lost to view. Then as the dinghy surged high on the next swelling roller they both caught a brief glimpse of the light. Almost instantly it flashed off again.

"Mat, quick, overboard," Rod cracked in a tense voice. "We'll have to swim for it. If there are Tiban guards hidden in those trees they'll probably spot the dinghy as it nears the shore."

Without hesitation Mat slid over the side, followed by Rod, who unsheathed a knife and slashed at the dinghy. Air hissed from the torn fabric as the craft crumpled up and floated sluggishly away.

"If—they find—it—washed up," Rod spluttered as he swam powerfully alongside Mat, "they'll figure it's—been wrecked—way out—at sea."

Shore-bound waves were now reaching high before thundering on to the beach. The two men, stroking in on crests, were suddenly hurled downward in a fury of tumbling foam, straight towards the deserted sands of the Tiban beach.

"Stay down," Rod called in an urgent whisper as, almost side by side, they swept chest down on to the beach.

Incoming waves poured over the two men. Rod ignored them while his eyes raked the shore and the tree-covered jungle beyond.

"Okay, Mat," he whispered at last. "Can't see anybody or anything. We've got to make those trees without being seen—I hope no one's about. Remember,

Barada's given orders to shoot on sight anybody landing on Tiba without his permission."

Mat made to rise to a crouch as though he was about to dash across the beach. Rod grabbed his arm and forced Mat down.

"We'll have to worm up the beach," he muttered in an undertone. "I'll lead, you follow. But first, slip off your jacket, tie it to your ankle and trail it behind you. That way we'll blur the tracks we make in the sand."

Flat on his chest, Rod began the slow, cautious crawl up the incline of the sandy beach. Using first one elbow, then the other, he inched steadily forward. Then, suddenly, he froze.

At his heels, Mat came to a halt, tensed and alert as he heard Rod's smothered hiss of alarm. "What is it, Rod?" he breathed anxiously.

"Land mines," came the startling reply. "The beach is mined. I've just uncovered one. Another move and my weight might have detonated it!"

Mat felt a prickle of fear down his

spine. What to do now—in a mine-field—in the darkness of the night?

Without warning, a beam of dazzling light burst across the beach to their left. Slowly, yard by yard, it began its sweep along the shore towards the spot where they lay.

Rod hissed over his shoulder, "Searchlight patrol. Must have been their flashlight we saw. Probably do a searchlight sweep once every hour. Just our luck to land when it's due."

The powerful beam crept steadily nearer. Rod darted a tense glance around him, but there was no cover on the open sands, not as much as a small rock. When the searchlight reached them it would pick them out as plainly as if they were two stranded whales.

"They won't stop to ask questions," Mat groaned grimly. "It'll be rapid fire—and curtains for us."

"Not while we're on the job," Rod rapped back. "Duck flat—then run for it when I give the word. We'll have to take our chance that we don't step on another mine."

While he spoke Rod was cautiously, but skilfully sliding his flattened palm under the soup-plate shape of the land-mine. Hardly

Cautiously Rod slid his hand under the land-mine.

daring to breathe for fear of detonating the murderous weapon, he lifted it clear of its shallow depression.

Mat lay quite still watching Rod, who, balancing the mine on his flattened hand, rolled on to his back, his outstretched arm at right angles to his body and flattened to the beach. Then with an immense heave, Rod pulled his body round sideways. His arm, flashing high, followed the swing of his body, and as it came towards the peak of its trajectory, the land-mine left his hand, curved through the air, and vanished into the dark.

C—RUMP—boo—m!

In a vivid flash of orange flame the land-mine exploded with a shattering roar, and a mountain of sand was blown skyward.

Even as the land-mine roared its destruction, Rod bellowed, "Up and run!"

Both men leaped to their feet and, bending low, legged it up the beach for the cover of the trees. Behind them the searchlight had whirled to focus on the sudden, thundering explosion. Next minute a crash of rapid firing echoed the land-mine's roar, and tracer bullets lit a murderous path to the sea. The probing searchlight prodded the darkness, searching for the cause of the exploding land-mine.

Rod, with Mat pounding at his heels, threw himself into a smother of bushes under the palms. "Near thing," he gasped. "The explosion held their attention just long enough for us to make cover. But it's alerted them that something's up. Now they'll have patrols out to seek the cause of the land-mine's blowing up."

"Our footprints in the sand——" Mat's voice trailed off into a groan. "And—oh, crikey——" he gasped in dismay. "My jacket. It must have come loose from my ankle as we sprinted up the beach."

"That settles it," Rod grinned ruefully at Mat. "Not your fault. But those beach patrol guards will know someone's bolted into the jungle when they see the prints and find your jacket. We've got to move—and fast."

Into the darkness of the jungle undergrowth they sped as fast as the thorny bushes and trailing vines permitted, while behind them came the sounds of pursuit. Darting quick backward glances, they saw faint lights dancing in the jungle as the armed patrols sought by flashlight for the mysterious invaders.

Before long, the jungle thinned, and Rod and Mat saw the shadowy outline of a newly made concrete track crossing their path. The undergrowth and trees had been cut back a few yards on each side of the track. Every hundred yards along its length and on both sides was a man-high upright post.

"We've got to cross that track," Rod panted as he came to a halt, at the same time casting a wary glance up and down the ribbon of concrete.

Mat made a move as if he was about to dart over the track, but Rod stopped him.

"Hold it," he ordered in an urgent, warning whisper. Mat eyed him wonderingly. "Strip to your underpants, and slip off your shoes."

Puzzled by Rod's startling command, Mat hurriedly and unquestioningly obeyed. He noted Rod eyeing the posts with grim intensity.

"And your wristwatch," Rod added as Mat completed his stripping and bundled his clothes together. "Toss 'em high in the air to the far side. Hurry! I can hear 'em breaking through the jungle."

Two bundles whizzed through the air over the bordering man-high posts and landed with dull plops on the scrubby verge on the far side of the track.

"Quick," Rod urged in a whisper. "Dash across the track and into the bamboos on the other side. Hurry."

Their stockinged feet made no sound as they pounded over the concrete and slid breathlessly into the bamboo grove.

The sound of thudding feet drew nearer, and the beams of flashlights splayed from the jungle across the concrete road. Bushes parted and a line of uniformed men crashed into view. Rod peered intently, and Mat heard a hiss of astonishment from his friend's lips.

"By heck," he breathed. "They aren't Tiban soldiers. Look, Mat! Those uniforms—they are the army dress of the East Power; and—see that flashlight—it's playing on some of their faces. Those soldiers are on patrol for the East Power."

Mat felt his pulses hammering. The

enemy searchers were less than fifty paces from where they were crouching. He shot a quick glance at Rod, who appeared to be unusually unperturbed. However his eyes betrayed his excitement. They flicked continually up and down the line of their armed pursuers, who had now halted at a command from an Eastern officer.

"By thump," Mat sighed in relief, "they are turning back into the jungle. But—why? Why don't they cross the track to hunt us out?"

"Because of those man-high posts," Rod gritted. "I figured when I saw 'em that they were electronic guards. If a man passes through those on to the track a warning is instantly flashed to a base patrol."

Still not completely convinced, Mat eyed the posts, then turned to Rod. "But surely any jungle animal passing between the posts would set off the electronic alarm," he whispered.

"No." Rod shook his head. "Animals don't carry metal on them. But all men do—knives, coins, studs in their shoes, rings or something metal. It's the metal which alerts the electronic alarm."

"I see." Mat eyed Rod admiringly. "So that's why you ordered me to strip, take off my shoes and watch, and throw the bundles *over* the posts."

The sound of the search could be heard receding into the distance and, gradually, the winking lights of the torches faded completely into the jungle. Mat gave a sudden, low smothered laugh as he and Rod scrambled swiftly into their clothes.

"Their clever guard posts have worked in our favour, thanks to you, Rod. They've fooled the chaps who put 'em up. Tricked by their own cunning," he chuckled.

Rod nodded and grinned as he turned to eye the track and its direction. One way it must lead inland, towards the centre of Tiba. But where did it go in the opposite direction? What was the reason for the narrow, concrete track? Why build it at all?

Brow furrowed in thought, he decided that the puzzle would keep until he had more time to think about it. Keeping his voice low he said in warning, "Keep clear of the posts. We're going to trail alongside the track to find out where it goes."

The night was silent except for the jungle

cries of unseen wild animals and the hum of insects. At a rapid pace the two men set off, keeping a wary look out for any signs of enemy guards.

"Why are the East Power soldiers in Tiba?" Mat muttered, as he hurried along at Rod's side. "And why has Barada ordered Britain to close the air base? He has always been friendly with Britain.

"That's what we're here to find out," Rod whispered back. "There's something mightily mysterious abroad in Tiba and whatever it is spells bad news for Britain," he ended abruptly as he came to a sudden halt.

Ahead of them the concrete track vanished into a thick grove of palm trees. Quickly making signals to Mat to follow him and make no sound, Rod skirted warily round the grove.

Suddenly, Rod gripped Mat's arm and pointed to the ground. The concrete path did not reappear on the far side of the palms.

"Rod, look!" Mat whispered and indicated a glow about half a mile away in the sky. "That light! What is it?"

"Must be the British air base," Rod replied in a low voice. "I think the boundary line must be just a few hundred yards farther on, through the jungle. The boundary was marked when Barada signed a treaty with Britain years ago. This track," and he turned to point back to where it vanished into the palm grove, "heads towards the line but stops short, and the end of it is hidden in the palm grove."

For what purpose was there a track at all? They both stared at the palm grove. Mat rubbed his chin in bewilderment. You could see that it had been recently constructed: but why?

Faintly at first but rapidly getting louder there came through the air a throbbing sound. At once, both Mat and Rod realised what it was—it was the steady drone of a heavy motor vehicle. Moments later, a large, canvas-topped, six-wheeled lorry rumbled into view along the track towards the palm grove.

Only its side-lights were on and these were carefully shielded to prevent the lorry being seen from the air. Slowly it rumbled on and out of sight into the grove. Next minute it stopped.

"Come on," Rod ordered grimly. "We're going into that grove. We'll go up to the far end, beyond the end of the line of guard posts."

Stealthily but swiftly the two friends edged past the tall palms and their thick skirting of jungle shrubs to a point beyond the line of guard posts. Soundlessly, they stole towards the grove with its slim, tall trees towering up into the night sky, and eased themselves into a position where they could see the back of the lorry.

"Ye gods!" Mat gasped in astonishment.

The lorry stood deep in the grove and at the end of the concrete track. The tail-board was down, and shadowy figures were busily off-loading crates and boxes and stacking them on to a platform. The platform and the boxes of food and supplies then disappeared into the ground.

"It's a loading lift," Rod whispered. "That means that there must be an underground building somewhere under the palms. But why? What is it there for?"

His searching gaze suddenly fastened on a

tall tree towering above its neighbours. It looked most peculiar and somehow out of place. Rod puzzled and frowned. There was something queer about it. Then he gave a hiss of astonishment and nudged Mat. As both men stared, the tree slowly turned round. From its base to its topmost fronds, the whole tree revolved.

Rod hissed, "It's a fake tree and a very cunning piece of camouflage it is too."

"But—but what's it there for?" Mat breathed, more in admiration than in fear.

"It's an enormously tall periscope, disguised as a tree to suit its surroundings," came Rod's swift reply. "And it's spying over the real, shorter palms at the British air base, which is about half a mile away on the other side of the treaty line.

Mat's eyes darted back to the lorry which was now completely off-loaded. The tailboard was being clipped back into place and the lorry crew were preparing to climb into the driving cab.

"That must have been supplies for the men living underground," Mat whispered.

Rod nodded. "Quick," he snapped. "We're going to find where that lorry came from. The spy-post watchers have gone down in the lift to their underground watch-room. Right, make a dash for it, and hop over the tailboard."

Both men sprinted for the rear of the slowly turning lorry which was about to make its way back along the track. With quick leaps they hurled themselves at the tailboard, hauled themselves upwards and dropped silently into the thick straw covering the floor.

"Sneak under the straw," Rod hissed in an urgent whisper.

The lorry rumbled steadily along the track for a little while, until, with a changing down of its gears, it slowed to a crawl. Rod slid from beneath the straw and poked his head cautiously over the tailboard and round the canvas wall of the body. He took a hurried peep.

"Mat," he whispered. "Gates ahead. The driver is slowing down to pass through. Come on, we've got to get off before it goes through the gates."

Astride the tailboard, both men were just about to drop to the ground when, from a

They sprinted to the rear of the lorry.

side track, the lights of a vehicle swung round on to the main track.

"Down," Rod ordered urgently and dived back under the straw, just as a jeep closed up rapidly behind, its lights illuminating the rear and inside of the bigger vehicle.

The lorry slowed to a walking pace and the jeep followed suit, its nose close to the lorry's tailboard. There was no escape for Rod and Mat until the jeep could overtake.

Suddenly, a man's voice yelled out a challenge, to which the lorry driver replied. There was the sound of gates being opened and the lorry jerked forward.

"We're through the gates," Rod whispered grimly. "We're in some sort of compound, I think."

The lorry halted, then began to reverse slowly. Shouted orders reached the two men where they lay concealed under the straw. There was a slight bump and the lorry stopped, and the driver and his mates dismounted. Rod cautiously parted the straw, only to replace it hurriedly over his head, before whispering to Mat.

"We've backed up to a ramp. The tailboard is being lowered, and the lights of a loading bay are shining into the lorry——"

The rest of his words were drowned by a harsh metallic clanking. Men on the loading ramp could be heard shouting instructions. The lorry shuddered. Something heavy was being cautiously loaded aboard.

Rod again stealthily parted the straw. What he saw froze every muscle in his body.

A tractor was backing on to the lorry, its massive steel caterpillar tracks chewing the straw into shreds. Slowly, steadily, the driver, his back to the British agents, reversed the machine on to the lorry's steel flooring, straight towards the spot where Rod and Mat lay flat under the straw.

Chapter Two

THE GRINDING caterpillars of the heavy tractor made the steel floor of the lorry shiver and vibrate. Crouched under the straw the two British security agents edged themselves backwards as the incoming tractor slowly thundered towards them.

Rod's brain raced. Unless they escaped before the massive tracks reached them, they would be crushed to death. They had only seconds left!

Thinking fast, his right hand darted to a pocket. Mat, peering at his friend through the straw covering, saw Rod flick the false top off his fountain pen and shoot a tiny pellet into the deep straw at the open end of the lorry.

Mat tensed. He knew what to expect—a second's exposure to air and the pellet would burst into flame.

Whoosh—a blaze of red fire surged up under the forepart of the tractor. The driver's yell of terror echoed through the air as he vaulted out of his seat, scrambled over the bonnet and leaped clear on to the loading bay. His frightened howls rent the night and above the din the two in the straw heard feet pounding towards the rear of the lorry.

Now that the rear floor was a mass of flaming straw, Rod leaped up, and with his sheath knife savagely slashed at the canvas covering at the front of the lorry until he had cut a man's-length slit.

"Out, Mat," he panted. "Quick, before the tractor blows up."

Mat darted to the slit and squeezed through. Rod thrust his own body after Mat's. At the other end of the now fast-burning vehicle, panicky men, their attention fixed on the fire, were rushing about with fire-extinguishers.

Dropping to the ground both men sprinted for the concealment afforded by a low-roofed building. Half-way there, Rod abruptly steered Mat aside and thrust him behind the cover of a pile of crates. Wordlessly, he pointed to the building.

At the only entrance to the squat structure stood a sentry, his eyes fixed on the blaze at the other side of the large compound. All the men who had been quietly moving about earlier were now excitedly prancing around shouting orders to one another.

"That sentry hasn't left his post," Rod muttered in a tense whisper. "It must be the commanding officer's headquarters of whatever this place is, Mat. Reckon we must take a look inside."

Mat flashed a glance over the building. The windows were shuttered and barred. No entrance that way.

Crouching behind a long line of piled-up boxes and crates, both men considered the situation. Finally, Rod poked Mat in the ribs and whispered, "I think I know a way to slip in unseen. Come on!"

Bending low, both men ran to the end of the line of crates. Reaching up, Rod pushed the top box away from them so that it fell with a crash to the front of the pile.

Peering between the crates they saw the sentry turn, startled. They could just imagine him staring vainly through the dark at the piled-up stores—the only light available was from the glare of the burning lorry. Rod pushed a second crate to the ground.

The sentry's weapon snapped up, pointing at the pile of boxes. They heard him shout in their direction. Mat smothered a low chuckle at the man's uncertainy. Rod pushed yet another crate off the top. It thudded to the ground.

The sentry's head turned left and right, but he was alone at his post. His fellow guards, being off duty, had run to the scene of the burning lorry. Rod encouraged his uncertainty and alarm by shoving a fourth box to the ground.

The two waiting men then saw the sentry slip a torch from his belt and begin to creep towards the line of crates. As he came nearer he focused the beam on to the tumbled crates, his rapid-fire rifle clutched ready for fast use.

"Right," Rod breathed. "Just to make him do what we want," and this time he pulled a crate to the ground so that it crashed loudly behind the pile.

At that, the bewildered sentry broke into a run to skirt round the pile. As he did so, Rod and Mat sped to the opposite end and rounded it. The pile of crates was now between them and the baffled sentry—and the unguarded door to the building was before them.

Doubled low they hurtled across the compound and flung themselves through the doorway. Rod darted a backward glance. The sentry had rounded the pile and his torch was fanning over the stretch of ground which the pair had just crossed.

"Okay, Mat," Rod breathed and grinned at Mat. "He hasn't a clue what's happened. Look—that door. There's a symbol on it which means it's the private office of whoever is the boss of this outfit. Let's take a dekko inside."

Cautiously Rod turned the door handle and pushed, but the door was locked. This pleased Rod. It meant the office was empty! In a flash he was slipping a slender length of strangely-toothed metal in the keyhole. A click—and the door opened.

The room was in darkness and the windows were shuttered, which meant there was no danger of a light being seen from outside. Without hesitation Rod felt for and found the light switch, and closing the door behind him, he flooded the room with light.

One glance told him what it was! The headquarters office of the commander of an army unit. But before the two agents could begin a search of his papers they heard the sound of a car engine approaching the building.

"No time to search the room," Rod snapped, and Mat watched while he swiftly clamped a tiny, circular object under the edge of the desk. Then they darted to the door. Rod clicked off the light and quietly opened the door a slit before looking down the passageway to the entrance.

"Must be the C.O. of this place," he murmured over his shoulder. "No chance to get out of the building; the sentry's back at his post. Come on, chum—it's up top for us."

Running in the opposite direction to the entrance, Mat hard on his heels, Rod sped round a corner just as the main entrance was flooded with light and booted feet stamped into the building. They heard men enter the commander's office—but, to their dismay, other heavy feet marched on along the passage.

Rod hurriedly felt one of the closed shutters, and finding the latch, silently swung the shutter open. Mentally he sighed with relief. The window had no bars. Climbing on to the sill, he pulled Mat up behind him and leaning out both men gripped the edge of the low roof above. In a flash they swung themselves up on to the flat roof. Rod leaned down and quietly swung the shutters back into place.

In the dark he pressed a tiny button on his wristwatch. Instantly, the micro-size receiver hidden in the watch emitted the sibilant sound of a voice talking angrily in East Power language.

"The transmitter button I stuck under the desk is working," Rod exclaimed, and Mat nodded with satisfaction.

"—searching for them now, and they must be found and shot——" The voice was cold with rage. The agents knew it was they to whom the speaker was referring. It brought a quiet smile to Rod's lips.

The voice was interrupted by the sound of a radio call signal from the room below.

Relayed to Rod and Mat through the hidden transmitter under the desk, it came through clearly.

"Palm grove to control," Rod's receiver whispered. The two British security agents tensed. This must be a radio message from the palm grove to the commander. "British spy plane taxiing for take-off. Urgent—urgent, repeat spy plane taking off. Palm grove out."

At once they heard the commander grate an order, and there followed the sound of hurrying feet in the office below. Then a loudspeaker roared an order which echoed over the compound outside.

"Black-out—black-out. All lights off."

"What goes on?" Mat hissed anxiously.

"The mob below don't want the British reconnaissance plane to spot this place," Rod rapidly explained. "So the commanding officer has relayed an order over the loudspeakers to black-out all lights until the recce plane has returned to its base. That's why that observation post with its camouflaged periscope is hidden in the palm grove—to spy on our base and report everything that goes on there."

"Including the take-off of our recce kites," Mat muttered, and Rod nodded.

Mat opened his mouth to say something but halted, mouth open, gaping at Rod. From Rod's micro-receiver came an ear-shattering scream. It pierced the silence of the night, echoing out from the roof across the darkened compound below.

Frantically, Rod switched off the tiny receiver; but he knew it was too late. Yells from the compound told them it had been heard and armed men could be discerned faintly in the darkness racing to surround the building.

"Your micro-receiver must have oscillated," Mat groaned in dismay. "Sounded like a screaming banshee."

"Wasn't the receiver," Rod growled. "It was the transmitter under the commanding officer's desk. Listen—they must have found it," and the furious shouts echoing up from beneath them proved Rod to be right.

"That's truly torn it," Mat grunted. "Now they know we've penetrated their hide-out. Listen, ladders are being put against the walls. Those armed thugs will be on the roof in a jiffy, Rod, winkling us out."

From the micro-receiver came an ear-shattering scream . . .

Rod was sweeping the flat top with a rapid gaze, searching for some place of concealment; but the roof was bare of cover except for a shallow, foot-high parapet wall which ran along its front end, and a small roll of forgotten roof-felt.

To Mat's amazement Rod darted to the roll of roof-felt, stood his pencil torch on end beside the roll and switched on the torch. A thin, powerful beam of light shot straight up, skywards. Rod leaped back alongside Mat.

"Lie flat against the base of that parapet wall," he hissed. "Crowd as close against it as you can."

Running to the wall, they flattened themselves against it, Mat's feet almost touching Rod's head. They had only just flopped down when men appeared over the parapet, crying out in astonishment and fury when they sighted the beam of light aimed to the sky, and the shadowy "figure" lying beside it.

With a rush they hurtled across the roof towards the torch. Mat needed no instruction from Rod. He whirled himself over the parapet, hung by his fingers and then let himself go. He landed with a light thud as Rod dropped beside him.

From the roof came angry shouts as the armed searchers discovered how they had been tricked. Their yells were answered from the compound, and Rod and Mat knew they were cornered. In the dark, whichever direction they looked, armed men were surrounding the building in an almost solid ring.

A powerful flashlight suddenly burst into their eyes, then was hurriedly switched off; but it was enough. They were caught! Rod's desperate bid to outwit the enemy searchers had failed.

An icy voice grated an order.

"Bring the prisoners inside!"

Rod expected to be marched with Mat into the commanding officer's room where he had planted the micro-transmitter. Instead, he and Mat were savagely thrust into another room. One glance warned them both that they were about to be tortured to force them to reveal why they had secretly entered forbidden Tiba.

For an instant Rod's thoughts flashed to Barada, the ruler of Tiba, who for years had been a warm ally of Britain. Was it possible that he was unaware of the East Power army in Tiba? As swiftly, he knew what the answer must be! Of course Barada knew! But—*why* had he so abruptly changed towards his old friends, the British? *Why* had he suddenly and secretly allied himself with Britain's most deadly enemy, the East Power? *Why* had he ordered the treaty to be ended and the British to vacate the air base on Tiba's farthermost tip?

Mat's gaze darted round their prison. His pulses quickened as his eyes fastened on a tight-lipped man, thickly spectacled, wearing a white overall coat. On shelves round the room were clustered bottles, jars and electrical instruments.

They were each pushed into a chair and their arms and legs strapped to it.

"You will now answer my questions," the man in the white coat began quietly, and the East Power commander, standing watching, nodded his head.

"Who are you and why have you come to Tiba?" white coat asked softly.

Rod eyed him scornfully. Mat's jaw set hard. Neither replied. Their questioner shrugged, picked up a metal plate, attached it to Rod's chair, then clipped a steel band to each wrist. He did the same to Mat.

Stepping to an instrument panel, he pressed a button. At once, a needle on a gauge began to quiver. Both men involuntarily tautened as a low current of electricity was passed through the bands into their bodies.

Slowly the needle climbed and as it did so the electric current increased steadily. Both agents felt their muscles quivering and it was as if every sinew in their bodies was being twisted. Grimly, they both battled to keep silent and still but the rising voltage was exerting a more vicious and stronger grip. They were rapidly becoming helpless in its power.

"Now, you answer," their torturer grunted, switching off the current. "That was a sample of what you both will suffer if you refuse. You will slowly, very slowly, be electrocuted! Not a pleasant ending, I promise you."

They were helpless prisoners. The man in the white overall meant what he said, and the East Power commander stared at them both with a ruthless, cruel gaze. Neither would have any qualms about murdering them if they refused to talk.

"Dead security agents are no good to Britain," Rod thought rapidly. "I've got to trick these two thugs so that we can stay alive—and complete our mission on Tiba."

"All right," he said in a voice into which he put a snarl implying defeat. Mat gasped when he heard Rod give in. He could hardly believe his ears. Was Rod about to betray the reason for their landing on Tiba?

What Rod said next shook Mat rigid! Had his friend, whom he had always looked up to and admired, suddenly gone mad—or yellow? Mat dismissed the thoughts as swiftly as they had come. But he stared at Rod in blank amazement as he listened.

"We've come to Tiba to assassinate Barada."

Rod appeared to be staring at the floor, his expression one of complete despondency. But, from under his lowered lids, he was keenly watching the others, and he saw them dart astonished glances at one another. He felt a thrill of excitement shoot through him.

Watched by the East Power commander,
the man pressed a button . . .

Would the commander take the bait Rod had skilfully laid? And would he fall for Rod's clever trick?

Abruptly the commander spun on his heel and marched out of the room. He was gone a while and when he returned he was accompanied by three tough men in uniform, guns in their belted holsters. He rapped out an order to them which brought a glint to Rod's eyes.

"The Barada is holding a garden party to-morrow evening in his palace gardens," the commander grated. "You will take these two white prisoners in secret to the palace garden where you will give this one," jerking a finger at Rod, "a revolver. He will shoot the Barada."

The commander stared at Rod malevolently and said triumphantly, "When the Barada's guests see what has happened they will tell the people of Tiba that a Britisher has slain their ruler. The people of Tiba will demand vengeance. They will send their army to attack the air base and drive the British into the sea."

He paused, then turned to the uniformed men and added with a cruel snarl, "If he fails, you will shoot him—and then you will shoot his companion. You can then tell the Barada that you men of the East Power have rescued him from two cunning, evil, British assassins."

Chapter Three

IT WAS the following evening. Darkness had fallen quickly and the palace gardens of the ruler of Tiba were glowing with soft lights. A band played and the Barada, a stately figure in his royal robes, stood next to a man in the uniform of Chief of Staff of the Tiba army.

Concealed behind a clump of bushes with their three tough warders, Rod and Mat viewed the scene before them. One of the armed men pulled Rod's sleeve and whispered, "There is the Barada of Tiba with his guests. Slip across the garden, but keep in the shadows until you are near enough to shoot at the Barada. If you don't kill him with your first shot, fire at him again." He thrust his aggressive face close to Rod's, "and if you fail to assassinate him, we will shoot your friend," and he pointed at Mat.

While the two other soldiers kept their guns trained on Rod, the third man pushed a revolver, barrel first, into Rod's hand. Rod was tempted to take the terrible risk of trying to shoot down all three, but he instantly dismissed the idea. Not only would they drill him before he could raise his weapon to the level of their chests, they would also slay the unarmed Mat in cold blood.

Rod flashed a gaze at the distant Barada, and the Chief of Staff at his side. His eyes narrowed. The Chief of Staff appeared to be staring directly towards the spot where the three murderous thugs and the British agents were hiding. Rod's gaze darted to the three soldiers, and he saw one of them flash a split-second signal from a pin-beam torch through the bushes to the Chief of Staff.

"By heck," Rod told himself, "this blighter is signalling Barada's Chief of Staff, alerting him we are here. That chap is a traitor to his ruler, Barada. He must be in with the East Power."

"Move, you," and Rod felt a gun dig into his ribs. "And remember, shoot to kill. Fail, and he gets shot," and Rod knew that Mat would die if he failed to obey.

Rod's teeth clenched. Just as he'd planned, his words had tricked the East

Power commander, but never had he expected that he would be ordered to assassinate the Barada. Now, if he failed, not only was his own life forfeit but that of the helpless Mat also.

The softly lit gardens of Barada's palace were full of guests strolling in the warm night. Above them, almost invisible, stretched the cables from which the lights were strung.

Rod stepped from behind the bush, his hand gripping the revolver in his side pocket. He stole stealthily towards the Barada who was now standing with his back to a large, ornamental pond. He knew the watchful eyes of the three guarding Mat were fixed on him.

He halted in the deep shadow of a large stone ornament. Barada was less than ten feet away. At his side the Tiba Chief of Staff swung his head round quickly and looked directly at the stone ornament, just as though he knew someone was hidden in its shadows. Abruptly, the Chief of Staff shifted his feet and moved a short distance away from Barada.

"That traitor *knows* Barada is about to

be assassinated," Rod fumed to himself. "And he's making sure he doesn't get in the way of a stray bullet."

Rod flicked a lightning look round the gardens. At that moment Barada was almost alone; his guests strolled around and the band had stopped playing. Rod's eyes darted to where Mat was held captive behind the bush, and he mentally measured the distance from himself to the bush.

Then, cautiously, and with grim care, he slid the gun from his pocket and took aim. Slowly, his fist steady and his brain ice-cool, Rod squeezed the trigger.

The shot crashed out in the still quietness of the night like a sharp clap of thunder—and in a moment the gardens were plunged into inky darkness.

Rod had skilfully shot up the distant fuse box, smashing the fuses and destroying the lights.

Even before startled, alarmed shouts began to echo round the garden, Rod was hurtling across the grass, shouldering bewildered guests aside as he raced to where Mat was held prisoner.

He burst through the bush and before the

startled armed thugs were aware of what was happening, his clenched fist and the gun butt were crashing into their jaws, sending them reeling to the ground.

"Run," he hissed to Mat, grabbing his arm and leading him back across the garden. When they reached the pond with its covering of water flowers, he pushed Mat in and dived in after him.

The flowered surface hid them, the large curled leaves allowing just sufficient room under their spread for Rod and Mat to keep their nostrils above water without being seen. Seconds later, the lights were restored.

Barada, looking confused and startled, was listening to the furious voice of his Chief of Staff when Rod, moments later, dared to raise his head sufficiently to see what was happening.

"Here is proof, Your Highness," the treacherous army chief was shouting, as he waved a photograph before Barada. "A photographer has just snapped this picture with his instant-picture camera. Look, your Highness. It is a photograph of a Britisher with a revolver taking aim to assassinate you."

Rod's eyes narrowed. So the treacherous Tiba general and his secret ally, the East Power commander had everthing laid on, even to planting a photographer with the latest type of instant-picture camera, to prove it was a Britisher who murdered Barada.

"If I'd done as I was ordered and assassinated Barada," he breathed in Mat's ear, "that picture would have been all that the traitorous general and the East Power needed to set Tiba in an uproar of vengeance against the British."

A figure slid up to the Chief of Staff, whispered to him and handed him a small box. Rod saw the Tiba general switch it on. At once, Rod heard his own voice.

"We've come to Tiba to assassinate Barada."

It was a tape-recording of Rod's phoney confession.

"What more proof do we need, Your Highness," the scheming Chief of Staff roared loudly, looking round at Barada's guests crowding close to see the photo and to hear the tape-recording. "The British planned to slay you, Highness. They must be driven from Tiba. I, your Chief of Staff, will give the order for our brave army to attack at dawn to throw them off our island."

A roar of approval came from the crowd but Barada shook his head as though disagreeing. The general, ignoring Barada, rounded on the crowd and shouted to them.

"The assassins must be found, and shot on sight." Howls of agreement rang through the gardens. The general raised his hand for silence. "Meanwhile, I go to alert our brave soldiers. At dawn, we attack the British air base," and before Barada could speak, the general strode away.

"Barada doesn't seem to like what his Chief of Staff intends to do," Mat hissed.

"But he looks powerless to stop him," Rod breathed back. "Mat, if the Tiba army attacks at dawn, as the crooked Chief of Staff plans, our chaps will fight back, and that is exactly what the East Power wants. Tiba would then squeal for help and the East Power would name Britain as an aggressor and come to Tiba's aid. It could start another world war."

In the gardens a furious search was going on for the two escaped "assassins". Rod and Mat crouching in the pond, peered from under the water flowers as uniformed figures probed every bush, swept flashlights into every tree and hunted through flower beds.

"Any moment some bright boy will think of searching this pond," Rod whispered. "Before that happens, we've got to scarper."

He froze. What he had just forecast was about to happen!

Two men in East Power uniforms had halted beside the pond, staring intently over it. Rod's lips tightened. They were two of the three armed villains who had forced-marched them to the palace gardens.

The daring agents were hidden inches only inside the retaining wall of the four-feet deep pond and within hand's touch of the pair now studying the flower-covered surface.

Cautiously Rod bent low, his hand probing the bottom until he found a heavy stone. Slowly he raised himself until his fingers were just clear of the water but still hidden by the water flowers.

Flexing his fingers he flicked the weighty stone across the pond. With a loud plop, the stone fell into the water at the far side of the pond.

Directly above the spot where the two agents crouched, the soldiers spun sideways to glare balefully at the spreading rings ruffling the surface of the water. For an instant their attention was distracted from the water's edge immediately in front of them.

Immediately, Rod shot upright in the water, his hands darted forward and each gripped an ankle of the two armed searchers. With a Herculean pull, he tugged them both into the pond. As they slid past him into the water, Rod grabbed each by the scruff of the neck and crashed their heads together, knocking them senseless.

It had all been done with hardly a sound and was over in seconds. Rod shot a look over the gardens. In the belief that they had escaped, the search for the two assassins had switched from the gardens, and now they were almost empty. Barada had been hurried into his palace for safety and put under armed guard by his Chief of Staff's orders—a cunning move on the general's part to prevent Barada countermanding his order and stopping the dawn attack on the British base.

"Drag 'em out," Rod ordered in a

whisper. "We'll strip them of their uniforms and weapons, then gag and bind them."

Expertly and swiftly the two unconscious East Power soldiers were stripped of their uniforms and hastily pushed out of sight under a bush. Quickly, at Rod's command, Mat donned one of the uniforms while Rod scrambled into the other. Finally, they strapped on the holstered gun belts. Mat shivered.

"Wow—all wet and chilly," he whispered. "Did we have to duck that pair before we borrowed their uniforms, Rod?"

"Shut up," Rod retorted with a grin. "The warm night air will dry 'em out. Come on. We've got a job to do."

He raced across the deserted gardens to the garden wall, where, just outside, the jeep which had brought them to the palace, was hidden. Clambering over the wall, both men raced to the jeep, Rod taking the wheel.

"Pull your peaked cap low over your face, Mat," he ordered, letting in the clutch. "In the dark it will hide the fact you are a white man."

"Where are we going?" Mat asked eagerly.

"Back to that compound," came the startling reply. "We're going to kidnap the East Power commander and get him over the treaty boundary into the British air base. If we succeed, maybe we can then prove that the East Power has a secret base on Tiba. When the world knows that, it will be enough to stop whatever plan it is up to in Tiba."

Mat gasped at the daring of Rod's plan.

"Switch on the jeep's radio receiver," Rod snapped. "May as well learn if any more radio signals are being flashed from the palm grove spy base."

They roared through the night and as the gates of the compound came in sight, both lowered their heads to hide their features from the sentry at the gate.

To their relief, he stepped aside and waved the jeep through into the compound. Rod and Mat were both thrilled. Was their plan going to succeed? Would they be able to seize the East Power commander, smuggle him out of his headquarters, race along the track and get past the hidden spy post to beat their way to the treaty boundary?

Rod was swinging the jeep round to park

it in the shadows of the headquarters building, when from the radio came a crackle followed by a voice speaking harshly.

"Alert—alert," all units. British spies escaped in jeep. Look out for stolen jeep. Spies believed to be wearing East Power uniforms. Spies are white Britishers. They must be caught and shot on sight. Alert—alert."

It was the voice of the Chief of Staff of the Tiba army! Rod felt a cold anger seize him. The man, sworn to loyalty to serve Barada, the ruler of Tiba, was a traitor to his country. He was in alliance with the East Power, aiding that ruthless force to achieve its cunning plan to seize control of Tiba.

From the gateway came a loud shout and Rod darted a glance back over his shoulder. The shadowy figure of the sentry was racing after them.

"Must have heard that broadcast over the guard-post radio," he gritted. "Out of the jeep Mat, and dive round the building out of sight."

They sped round the headquarters building, but the sentry had seen them vanish and his loud yells were bringing others running to join him.

"Look," Rod panted. "That patrol," and he pointed to a line of men marching two abreast in the dark ahead of them, about to enter what seemed to be a tunnel. "Quietly, Mat, slip in behind 'em and join on the end of the patrol. Snap to it."

On tip-toe they sped after the marching men. Behind them they could hear the pounding feet of the sentry and the other soldiers who had run from the building and loading bay.

Rod and Mat slipped quietly on to the rear of the column and fell into step with the men in front. They kept their heads tucked down on their chests. One of the two men immediately in front of the two agents glanced back and Rod saw his look of surprise.

Before he could ask a question, Rod forestalled him.

"Eyes front," he hissed in a guttural whisper. "Don't give us away. We're late on patrol," and the other uttered a low grunt of amusement as he faced front again.

Mat threw Rod a quick grin of admiration. Once again his lightning-witted friend had fooled the enemy! However, his thoughts sobered as, from the rear, a torch beamed and swept over the patrol.

From under their peaked caps, Rod and Mat slid anxious glances sideways. The sentry was running in the direction of the patrol, followed closely by about twenty other men. The sentry was carrying a torch, which he was focusing on the marching column.

"Two white spies are in the compound," he bellowed. "Have you seen them?"

They saw the man who had glanced back at them stiffen. The sentry's startling question had alerted him, and his suspicions were aroused! He half-turned, to stare directly into the faces of the pair behind him.

Thinking quickly, Rod gripped Mat, spinning him half-round and away from the man in front as he pointed to the distant line of crates they had previously used as cover.

"Two men ran behind those boxes," he

called truthfully, but did not add that it was he and Mat who had run behind them —the night before.

The pursuers swept round and hared off in the direction Rod was pointing. The man in front of them had halted while his companion in the column and the rest of it marched on. From out of the shadowy darkness near the head of the marching patrol an order roared.

" Get back into column, back there."

The East Power soldier jerked round and sped to fall into step. Rod breathed with silent relief. It had been a near thing, but his swift resourcefulness had saved them from disaster. But they were not yet out of the wood, and he urged Mat hurriedly forward to the tail of the patrol, which was now entering the tunnel opening.

The tunnel was in darkness, but someone up in front had flashed on a powerful torch and was leading the patrol down a sharp incline. Rod put out his hand and felt the tunnel wall. It was rock. They were inside a hill, descending into its depths.

Where was the patrol going? And why?

In the darkness, while he and Mat kept

in step with the marching feet ahead, Rod's thoughts flashed back to Barada. His first sight of the ruler of Tiba had been in the palace gardens, and Rod's picture of him was of a kindly, honest man. Why, then, had he so abruptly turned against his allies and friends, the British?

Rod's thoughts were brought to a sudden stop. The column had emerged from the tunnel and had halted on the bank of an underground river flowing blackly through the hill.

The man with the torch splayed light on a long canoe which was moored alongside the rocky bank.

"On board, one by one," a voice barked.

The leading pair climbed cautiously into the bow of the long craft. It swayed to and fro. The soldier with the torch snarled a warning and Rod guessed he was a senior n.c.o. in charge of the mysterious patrol.

"Board carefully," he grated. "A canoe overturns easily. Right, the next pair, get aboard," and two more men slithered into the canoe, squatting down behind the first two.

"Can we smoke, sir?" a voice pleaded.

To Rod's surprise the n.c.o. snapped his consent.

"No fear of lights being seen by a spy plane down here," he growled loudly. "So if any of you want a smoke, you are allowed to do so."

At once, some of the shadowy figures on the bank, waiting their turn to board the canoe, could be seen eagerly searching for their cheroots. The man who had almost discovered Rod and Mat put one to his lips.

They saw him strike a match on the sole of his boot. Its flaming head snapped off and shot like a miniature rocket towards the roof.

Instinctively, Mat's eyes lifted to follow the bright trail and in its brief flame the man who had struck the match looked full-faced at Mat.

He let out a startled shout.

"The white spies—they are here!" and his gun whipped out to cover Rod and Mat.

Chapter Four

ROD AND MAT were caught unawares by the sudden, dismaying accident of the lighted match. The East Power soldier's shout echoed furiously in the tunnel. In a moment his companions were surging excitedly towards him, eager to seize the two daring white spies.

Finger on trigger, the man pointed the gun steadily at Rod and Mat. The n.c.o. who had been at the front end of the patrol, burst through the soldiers to take charge of the dramatic capture. This would be a terrific triumph for him—he might get a medal.

He thrust himself forward, his torch clearly illuminating the white skins and British features. Rod watched his excited approach intently.

"Get your hands raised," the n.c.o. screamed, pushing his torch into Rod's chest.

This was what Rod was waiting for. Up shot his arms—his hand struck the held-out torch and it swivelled round to shine into the eyes of the man covering them, dazzling him for a brief instant.

Rod pushed Mat into the underground, darkened river and dived after him. Propelling himself underwater alongside the canoe, he heaved himself upwards and turned it over, hurling the boat's four occcupants into the water.

He swept back alongside Mat.

"Swim under the upturned canoe," he hissed, and both men streaked below the surface towards the canoe, now floating away from where it had been moored. Rod's tremendous heave to capsize the craft had broken its moorings.

Together they surfaced under the overturned canoe. They could hear the infuriated yells of the n.c.o and his patrol on the bank and the howls from those in the water.

"They won't dare open fire 'cos of the chaps in the drink," Rod chuckled. "And they aren't likely to drill the canoe because they need it—once they've got it back."

Floating under the upside-down craft, they drifted with the current at a rapid pace. They were in complete darkness and could not see where the river was taking them.

The gun was pointed steadily at Rod and Mat . . .

Once again, Rod used his sheath knife, to cut two tiny peep-holes in the prow.

"We're still in the tunnel," he muttered, peeping through the holes. "Can't see anything except its inky dark. Wait—there are lights dead ahead."

Swiftly the river swept them towards the lights. Rod tensed. Because of the lights, he could now see and what he saw brought a low whistle of dismay from him.

"Those lights come from a guard-post, Mat. The tunnel opens out a little and there's a path running alongside the water. By thunder, they are lowering weighted nets into the water. They must have been alerted by radio to look out for us," Rod groaned in dismay.

"What's the idea of the nets?" Mat gasped.

"Must be to catch anything—or anybody," Rod corrected himself grimly, "floating downstream. It will halt this capsized canoe, for sure, and they will hook it to the bank and right it."

The swift current was sweeping the canoe rapidly towards the net. The lights were from wide-angle lamps on the bank, and they bathed the river in a light as bright as day. Rod knew it was impossible to sneak ashore and up the rocky bank without being spotted by the guards, now only a few yards ahead.

"Dive," he ordered. "We've got to get under that net. Go to the bottom."

Kicking downwards they sighted the net and its lead weights anchoring it to the underground river's rocky bottom. Rod fingered the net, the lights from above giving sufficient murky light for him and Mat to be able to see.

Raising the net at its centre, Rod wriggled under and held it up for Mat to follow. Mat kicked his way beneath it—and suddenly stopped, mouthing an urgent message at Rod. He was trapped, something was holding him from getting through!

Rod's chest ached with holding his breath and he knew Mat must be in the same grim predicament. They could not stay down much longer. They would *have* to surface for air very soon—or drown!

But Mat was trapped—a prisoner held down by the net. Rod, his eyes glazing with the desperate effort to retain air in his lungs, battled with the net; but whatever it was gripping Mat would not let him go.

Then, suddenly, Rod's frantically probing fingers discovered the snag; the bayonet scabbard in the belt of the East Power uniform was entangled in the mesh of the net.

Snatching his sheath knife from its casing, Rod slashed furiously through the belt's webbing, cutting it free from Mat's waist. Mat was free but, as though to mock them both, the belt floated gently upwards.

Desperately, both men kicked downstream, their chests heaving with the fearful need for air. But they dare not surface to the harsh glare of the guard-post lights above. The swift current aided them downstream and, seconds later, they surfaced, and with great intakes of air refilled their lungs.

A clamour arose from the guard-post. The slashed belt had floated to the surface and been seen at once. Instantly, the guards guessed the two British dare-devil security agents had slipped the net and escaped downstream.

Rod and Mat glanced quickly backwards. The guards, armed with Sterling rapid-fire weapons, were tearing along the path beside the underground river. Rod knew they had no chance of outstripping the pursuers while they remained swimming in the river.

"But the second we climb the bank they'll sight us," Mat gritted, "and drill us with their Sterlings."

Rod fumbled in an inner pocket in his borrowed uniform and extracted a grey pellet from its container. He gave it a quick squeeze and felt it crack before he hurled it as far back up-river as he could.

The pellet dropped on to the bank, and from it came a cloud of dense, choking smoke which swelled up into the air and hid their pursuers.

Exhausted, the two swimmers drew themselves out of the water, clawed themselves up the bank and began to race along the rocky pathway under the overhead roof of the tunnel.

"Rod, we're trapped," Mat gasped as he skidded to a halt. The tunnel ended up against what appeared to be a blank wall of solid rock. The river swept onwards into a huge pipe, its mouth covered by a thick metal grating.

The smoke back along the underground river tunnel would not hold the enemy for long. Once it thinned sufficiently, the soldiers of the East Power guard-post would pursue them at full speed.

"We've got to get out of sight somehow," Mat urged in a desperate voice, while both raked the tunnel with searching eyes, seeking some crack in the rocks in which to conceal themselves.

"Look, Rod," Mat gritted. "There's a ledge above the path, near the roof."

"No good, Mat," Rod shook his head. "If we can see it, so will they. You can bet your life they will search every inch if they don't spot us immediately."

"Then——" Mat drew a deep breath, "we'll have to try to hide in the river, diving under when they get here."

For answer, Rod pointed upstream, his jaw set grimly. Mat stared in the direction he was pointing and gasped.

Below the surface of the water was a light, two lights, then more, deep down and approaching slowly along the bed of the river. Mat stared in astonishment, puzzled and tense with anxiety.

"Frogmen," Rod snapped. "With headlights on their helmets. They're searching the river for us—or our bodies," he added grimly.

"Listen," Mat whispered, and from back up-river the pounding of feet could be heard coming nearer and nearer.

Mat's eyes darted to Rod. What could they do? The frogmen were nearing the point where the river swept through the grill-barred pipe. There was no escape that way! And within a few more moments the East Power killers would come into sight along the rock path above the river. There was no way out for them this time! They were cornered!

"Strip that East Power jacket off," Rod rapped, ripping off the tunic he was wearing and rebuttoning it swiftly. Mat did the same with his, tense with sudden hope that Rod was, once again, about to outwit the enemy.

"Hurry, Mat, tie the end of the sleeves, and fill 'em with these loose lumps of stones and rock. And bung the side pockets full, also."

Frantically they pushed the chunks of stone and rock lying on the path into the knotted sleeves and pockets. The approaching feet were not far distant. The flash of torch beams could be seen as the seekers of the British agents probed the path ahead with their flashlights.

"Drop 'em into the river, so they fall midstream or thereabouts," Rod ordered urgently.

He tossed his stone-weighted tunic out and across the water. It fell almost midstream and he saw it sink in a cloud of bubbles. Mat did not hesitate. He instantly copied Rod.

"What's the idea, Rod?" he gulped.

"You'll see—if it works," was the hurried retort. "Quickly, Mat, up on that ledge, and lie flat and quiet."

Mat leaped at the ledge, his fingers closed on the rim, and with a heave he pulled himself flat on to it, then leaned over to haul Rod up alongside.

Lying there, they cautiously peered over the ledge. Below, in the depths of the river, the approach of the frogmen's helmet lights could be seen; and on the river bank, the enemy searchers burst into view.

As they watched from their perch the two saw the leading light in the water below, come to a halt. The other lights steered towards it. Rod's eyes glinted. One of the frogmen had discovered a tunic on the river bed, and was pushing upwards through the water. Next moment he broke the surface, waving his arm above his head, and yelling as he dragged his mouth mask aside.

The guards on the bank came to a halt, and gathered in a bunch above the frogman. Rod and Mat saw him point downwards.

"He's telling 'em he's found the tunics," Mat breathed, but Rod ignored the remark.

"Work your way back along the ledge," he hissed. "Don't make a sound, but make all the speed you can. Hurry, Mat, hurry."

Startled by Rod's astonishing command to return the way they had come, only by way of the ledge, Mat did not question his friend. In silence, as fast as he dared and taking care not to loosen a stone or send a stray pebble tumbling from the ledge to the

The frogman had spied one of the stone-filled tunics . . .

path below, Mat wriggled along the ledge, hardly daring to breathe.

The guards, peering down at the lights of the frogmen in the depths of the river, were right below the two men.

Foot by foot, Rod and Mat edged backwards, every muscle strained and tensed, knowing that one tiny sound from them would be caught instantly by the sharp ears of the enemy only a few feet below them.

Once again the frogman broke the surface, this time clutching one of the tunics, which he tossed on to the bank. At once, the guards snatched at it. A howl of fury broke from them when they discovered the jackets were weighted with rocks and stones. A moment later a second frogman surfaced, and threw the other rock-loaded tunic ashore.

" Faster, Mat," Rod whispered. " Got to put as much distance as we can between us and them before they resume their search for us."

The ledge curved round a slight bend in the tunnel, and they were out of sight of the frogmen and the guards on the underground river bank. In a flash, Rod dropped from the ledge to the path, followed by Mat.

"Back up the path," Rod whispered. "On your toes."

Soundlessly they sped along the path until they reached the next curve. Rod halted, listening.

Infuriated shouts reached them. Rod's lips curved in a tight smile. The raging searchers had discovered that they had been tricked. Rod heard the n.c.o. of the enemy guards bellow an order.

"Search that ledge, and shoot 'em on sight. They must be hidden up there."

The scrabble of feet on rock reached them, then came a shout.

"Not up here!"

"Phee-ew!" Mat gasped. "That was smart—to hold their attention, while we slithered back along the ledge. You completely fooled 'em, Rod."

Rod stilled him with an urgent sign. The n.c.o. was yelling another order.

"The High Command must be alerted," he roared savagely. "The British spies have slipped us. They must have got through to the secret base. At the double, march."

The tramp of marching feet hurrying

away from them echoed along the tunnel Mat threw a startled glance at Rod.

"They are marching at the double straight for that solid wall of rock at the end of the path!" he exclaimed.

"Yes, sounds like it," Rod agreed. "I figure we'd better do some trailing to see what happens when they reach it. Brr-rr; it's cold down here!"

Both of them were in wet clothing, and it would be good to be on the move once more to stir their blood and drive the chill out of their limbs.

They broke into a silent trot which soon began to warm them. Rod warned Mat to take care not to tread on loose rocks or pebbles. They must make no sound. A faint glimmer from the far end of the tunnel helped them to avoid stony patches on the rocky river path.

Rod signalled to Mat to slow down. The marching feet ahead of them, hurrying at double-time marching, were now nearer. The trotting agents had rapidly overhauled their quarry. They fell into a quick walk, alert for any soldiers who might have been left to guard the path.

"—Sss!" Rod, in the lead, hissed Mat to a halt.

They were on the turn of a long bend. At the far end of the bend the East Power men whom they were silently trailing had come to a stop in front of the solid wall at the end of the tunnel.

The n.c.o. of the patrol was at the front of his squad and hidden from Rod and Mat, who crouched against the wall a hundred yards in the patrol's rear.

"Give me a hoist," Rod whispered.

Mat cupped his hands together at knee-height. Rod put one foot in them. Mat lifted and Rod, putting his palms flat against the rock wall of the tunnel to steady himself, was hoisted high enough to see over the heads of the distant group of enemy soldiers.

The n.c.o. was grasping a slim steel instrument. Rod saw him tapping a button on it with his forefinger as though he was morsing a radio signal. Rod slid to the ground.

"The n.c.o. is operating a radio bleeper," he whispered. "Sending a signal."

The patrol was standing to attention.

"Looks as if they're waiting for something

to happen," Mat muttered in a perplexed whisper.

"Yes, and there it is," Rod rapped.

The rock wall at the end of the tunnel shot up silently, revealing an inner tunnel. Immediately, the patrol, led by its n.c.o marched into the inner tunnel. As they did so, a sudden blaze of dazzling light burst from the far end.

"Thunder!" Rod gasped. "There's a massive vault of some sort at the end of that inner tunnel, Mat. A door must have opened at the far end and the blaze of light is coming from that vault."

Tensely, they watched the patrol vanish through the inner tunnel into the vault at the far end. As the last men passed through into the brilliantly lit vault, its door slid across behind them.

Without a word Rod and Mat broke into a run and sped to where the rock wall had opened up to reveal the inner tunnel. They halted, eyeing it.

"The n.c.o. must have operated the outer door with his radio bleeper's code signal," Rod breathed to Mat. "Looks as though he forgot to bleep it down behind his patrol."

He made to step under the raised doorway, when he froze, his eyes fastening on what looked like two tiny glass buttons, one on either side of the doorway. The buttons were outside the tunnel entrance.

"Don't move, Mat," he hissed in hasty warning.

But he was a split second too late.

In his eagerness to investigate the secret tunnel and the door at its far end, Mat had darted forward.

CLANG!

With a dull, metallic thud, the secret section shot down behind Mat.

The glass buttons concealed an invisible electronic beam. Anyone passing between them broke the beam and set in motion an electric relay which instantly closed down the secret door.

Mat was a prisoner, trapped inside the inner tunnel.

Chapter Five

Rod stared blankly at the closed secret door. It was cunningly camouflaged to look like a part of the end wall of the tunnel, and it was not surprising that he and Mat had failed to detect it earlier that night.

But behind it, Mat was imprisoned. Rod's jaw tightened. By now Mat was probably in the hands of the East Power enemy troops. Rod was certain there was a warning system which would inform those inside the huge lighted vault when the beam was broken.

He thought furiously and came to a rapid conclusion. If they had captured Mat, they would know he was one of the two white men being hunted. They would then guess the second white man was not far away! Any moment now the outer door might shoot up and armed men pour from the inner tunnel in search of him!

Already Mat had been behind the secret door for at least a minute. Instinctively,

Rod darted a glance at his watch. He smothered a groan of dismay.

In three hours it would be dawn! Then, the treacherous Chief of Staff of Barada's army and the soldiers of Tiba would launch a sudden attack on the British air base.

Unless that attack was halted and the Tiban troops stopped before they could reach the treaty boundary line, the British would be defending their base against the Tiban army. Rod was grimly aware of what would happen then. The traitorous Chief of Staff would call for immediate aid from his secret ally, the East Power, to "defend" Tiba against the British "invaders".

If that happened, Rod knew there was the most terrible risk of the battle of Tiba triggering off a world war!

Only he and Mat could prevent it. Only they knew the truth. But Mat was a prisoner behind that secret door; and he, Rod, had no means of rescuing him, nor of alerting the British base to put it on its guard before dawn in three hours' time.

Rod was desperately searching for some way of breaking through the secret door when he touched what seemed to be a thin line. It ran just above the height at which the top of the doorway would come. He felt along it quickly, his pulses racing with excitement!

The thin line was, in fact, the edge of a steel girder set into the rock face. Rod guessed it must be the lower edge of the steel slot up which the door slid out of sight. The girder ran the full width of the hidden door and protruded not more than ten inches from the rock face. Like the door, it was camouflaged to look like the rock in which it was inserted. Only Rod's searching inspection had detected it!

"Any second that door is going to shoot up, and armed East Power thugs pour out to hunt me," he gritted under his breath.

He reached up and gripped the camouflaged girder. Pulling himself up until his jaw was above the level of the girder, he swung his right leg up and hooked it on to the girder.

Pressing his right knee hard down on to its top surface, Rod strained until his muscles bulged as he forced his body to rise until he could get his right shoulder on to the steel support. Gripping the edge with his outstretched left hand, he held himself in a precarious horizontal position along the girder.

"Can't hang on for long," he thought desperately, the weight of that part of his body now on the narrow support threatening to throw him off. "But must do so—only hope of rescuing Mat, *and* escaping to alert the base."

Without warning the door below him shot up. He could hear it sliding upwards behind the girder on which he was stretched precariously at full length.

Out from the tunnel poured half a dozen men, each gripping a rapid-fire gun and their leader a blazing torch.

Rod held his breath, fearful that the thug with the torch might spin round and flash it upward.

The torch-bearers halted and waved the powerful beam to and fro along the wall of the river tunnel, then at the river itself, and finally at the steel grating covering the river's entry into the pipe.

The men behind the leader stepped clear of the door through which they had come.

From his hidden perch Rod saw that light was glimmering out of the tunnel. His alert brain told him that the inner door of the mysterious lighted vault must be open.

In an instant a plan flashed into his head.

The East Power soldiers had moved forward along the path by the underground river, probing every crack and crevice in the rock wall in a furious search for Rod.

Silently he eased his body off the girder and, fingers gripping the edge of the steel, let himself swing in the doorway to the inner tunnel. With a quick glance to right and left he noted quickly the position of the two tiny glass buttons which operated the electronic beam.

Cautiously he let his fingers slip a little and swung his body forward until his feet swept through the invisible ray, breaking it. Instantly, he felt a vibration through the girder.

Rod swung himself forcefully forward, at the same time releasing his grip of the girder above.

His body swept through the opening; his head narrowly missing the rapidly descending secret door. As he hurtled to the floor of the inner tunnel he heard the door clang shut behind him.

"I was right," he gasped. "That beam is set so that it works only when it's been broken twice. The first time it's broken is when someone goes through, either to enter or leave the inner tunnel. When he returns and breaks it for the second time, it sets the relay in action which closes the door behind him."

How long it would be before the locked-out n.c.o. would use his bleeper's secret radio code to open the door, Rod did not know. But the thought spurred him to swift action.

Light blazed into the inner tunnel from the far end. The door separating the tunnel from the vault was open, ready for the returning East Power searchers when they came back with their prisoner! Rod smiled grimly. They weren't going to find him back along the river. Instead, he had stolen a march on them and beaten them back into their secret hide-out!

He crept to the open door and cautiously peeped through. His eyes widened at what he saw!

Rod's feet swept through the invisible ray . . .

The vault was much larger than he had expected it to be. Before him was a vast, concrete, underground building with an enormous floor expanse. He stared at the floor and frowned in puzzlement. It was of steel and the centre section seemed to be mounted on rollers—as if the wide middle could roll apart to reveal a long, wide gap.

All round the sides of the vast floor men in overalls and field service caps were at work with the machinery—lathes, capstans, winches, machine tools, and electric generators. Rod's astonished gaze swept over them and then darted upward. An overhead gantry ran from one end of the long, windowless, reinforced building to the other. A powerful, overhead travelling crane was mounted between the gantry, ready to lift and transport heavy machinery up or down the immense workshop.

Rod turned to eye a steel-floored gallery running along one side of the mysterious underground place. Fronting and running the full length of the gallery was a glass-fronted office. It was a blaze of light.

Gripped between two armed East Power soldiers, and facing a man in the uniform of a high-ranking officer, was Mat, his back to the glass windows of the office. The window behind that was open.

Rod tensed. As he watched from his hiding-place inside the doorway of the tunnel, it was clear to Rod that Mat was being questioned by the officer. Suddenly, the officer raised his hand and struck Mat a violent blow on the face.

Rod bit his lip, temper rising up in him like a flood-tide. "Mat must have refused to answer that ugly blighter's questions."

Once more the officer raised his hand, but this time it was to point at an electric clock on the wall above him. Rod's eyes followed the officer's hand and he stiffened. Two and three quarter hours to dawn! That was when the treacherous Chief of Staff would launch his surprise attack on the British air base.

With another quick glance round the vast, underground workshop, Rod reckoned there would be about two to three hundred East Power technicians working here on steel casings and other metal parts. With all this secrecy what else could they be but parts for war weapons.

"An underground armaments factory," he whispered to himself. "But how did the East Power smuggle all that machinery into this subterranean vault? The only entrance is through this small door."

His eyes flashed round the grim scene once more, at the machines, at their operators in East Power army overalls, at the mysterious roller-mounted section of steel flooring and, finally, at a wired cage division lined with steel racks. The door leading into the wired-off section bore a large red warning, DANGER. It was the store for the completed armaments and Rod saw that it housed bombs, fuses, grenades and mortar missiles.

Switching his eyes back to the glass-fronted office up on the steel-floored gallery, Rod saw Mat stagger back from yet another furious blow delivered by the officer.

Rod clenched his teeth. He must rescue Mat before that brutal East Power officer could do him a fatal injury. Judging by the savage expression on the officer's snarling face, he was on the point of striking the defiant Mat with the butt end of a rifle which he had snatched from one of the guards.

Rod jerked up one of the legs of his slacks

o reveal a watertight polythene bag strapped o his calf. Swiftly he broke the seal on the ag and whipped out an alloy tube. Into he base he rapidly screwed a tiny capsule f compressed air and into the tube itself he ropped an inch-long metal dart. Lastly, e clipped a miniature rifle sight and micro-elescopic lens on to the tube which he raised o eye level, and taking quick, true aim, riggered the compressed air capsule.

The faintest hiss of air zipped from the ube as the dart flashed at lightning speed hrough the open window and over Mat's ead. It pinned itself on to the wall above nd behind the raging officer who was bout to smash the rifle butt into Mat's jaw.

Desperately, Rod snatched a thumb-sized radio transmitter from the polythene bag and flicked its volume lever to full, down to alf-volume, then back to full. Over and over again he did this.

The dart pinned on the wall was a micro-receiver, and as Rod oscillated his transmitter at full power there came from the dart a deafening, high-pitched wail. The sound rose and fell in a scream as Rod turned

the volume to full, down to half, the
back again.

The noise was exactly like a siren and t
all army units, in all armies throughout th
world, that siren wail means one thing only

ACTION STATIONS!

Coming from the office of the commande
of the underground armaments factory th
screeching wail alerted the hundreds o
overalled technicians on the steel floor below

Dropping their tools, they hurtled to point
where their weapons were stacked or hung
Everywhere, men, stirred to alarm by th
warning siren-like howls, were dashing to
snatch their arms and race to their actio
stations.

In the general mêlée, Rod threw himsel
from the doorway, across the steel flooring
up the steps to the gallery and came to a
halt outside the open door of the office. In
his hand he clutched a glass ball.

"Mat, eyes shut tight," he thundered, as
he hurled the glass ball into the office.

There was a tinkle of smashing glass and,
as Rod himself squeezed his eyes tight shut,
a blinding, flaring, dazzling burst of red
light filled the office.

Cries of fear filled the room. Rod opened his eyes. The men gripping Mat had released their holds, their hands frantically covering their eyes. The officer dropped the rifle he had been about to use on Mat and, staggering back, was shrieking in terror while he wiped at his eyes.

Rod leapt into the room and grabbed Mat.

"C'mon," he gritted. "They'll recover from that flash in a few jiffies. Before they do we've got to vanish."

As they fled from the office, Rod flashed a hurried look over the gallery rail. The men below had not seen what had happened in the office, but were still moving about the floor seeking their action stations and Rod could see there was no escape back to the tunnel. A squad of armed men were covering it.

"The gantry," he hissed. "Up that girder, Mat, on to the gantry trolley track."

The girder rose from the steel floor below, up past the gallery, and finished near the roof, and it helped support the steel rail track along which the overhead crane travelled.

There was a burst of red light as Rod leapt . . .

Unseen by the scurrying East Power men on the floor below, Mat and Rod raced up the girder and whipped over the edge of the rail track stretched beneath the roof.

" Flatten out along the track," Rod panted in a whisper. " It's just wide enough. They won't be able to see us from below. We'll lie up here while they rake the building for us."

A whistle shrilled through a loudspeaker. Instantly, every man came to attention. From the loudspeaker snarled the angry voice of the commander.

" Return to your duties immediately. Squad Party, search for two white spies. They are hidden in our secret base. Kill them."

Cautiously, the two peeped over the edge of the gantry track. Rod was stretched along it with Mat behind him. Down below, the overalled men were replacing their weapons and speeding back to their machines, while a group in East Power uniforms split into pairs to begin the hunt for the two, daring fugitives.

Mat gripped Rod's ankle. Rod twisted

his head. Mat was jerking a thumb towards the far end of the floor below.

Four of the searchers were manœuvring a telescope trolley into position. While the friends watched tensely, two of the soldiers, grasping rapid-fire guns, climbed aboard the trolley's platform. The other pair operated the trolley-lifting controls.

The telescopic framework began to rise, the two armed men standing on the platform back to back, their eyes raking the building from end to end as the platform rose steadily higher and higher.

" When that platform reaches its summit, it will be right up in the roof," Mat hissed through his teeth. "They can't fail to spot us then, Rod. We will be a pair of sitting ducks for their rapid-fire rifles."

Foot by foot, the trolley's platform crept upward. Rod and Mat, grim-faced, watched its steady progress when, suddenly, the track on which they lay began to tremble.

Rod's eyes flicked upwards from the rising platform to the travelling crane suspended between its twin tracks. It was moving slowly towards him, rolling almost soundlessly on its broad steel wheels. Slowly, remorselessly, it crept along the track to the spot where Rod and Mat lay in its path.

If they remained where they were, the steel wheels would crush them to death. If they leapt from the track to the steel gallery below, they would be seen instantly by the men on the slowly-rising platform, whose rapid-fire weapons were at the alert, ready for deadly action!

Chapter Six

THROUGH grimly set lips, Rod breathed tensely, while he cast a desperate look at the slowly advancing crane and the steadily rising platform. Down below, the East Power men in overalls were all stooped over their machines, unaware of the tense drama taking place above them.

"Rod!" Mat hissed at his pal. "Look down into the office."

In spite of their awful danger Rod took a quick glance through the windows of the office below them.

The commander of the East Power secret underground arms factory was gesticulating furiously while he talked to another officer in the uniform of a high-ranking officer.

But it was not the uniform of an East Power officer!

The man to whom he was angrily talking was the Chief of Staff of Barada's army. It was clear to Rod that the East Power commander was raging about the two daring

British security agents who had, so far, outwitted him and his men.

He jerked a finger at the clock. Rod saw the other turn to look up at the clock, and then nod, as though he was reassuring the East Power commander that everything was as planned.

As planned! Rod flashed a hurried look at the clock. It would be dawn in about two hours—time for the treacherous attack on the British air base.

The track beneath Rod vibrated with increasing tremors. Mentally, Rod measured the distance between the slowly advancing travelling crane and Mat and himself. In less than two minutes the wheels of the crane would bear down on them.

The platform, with its cargo of two armed snipers, was less than five feet below the level of the gantry track.

Taut with desperation, Rod sought for a way of escape from their deadly predicament.

Suddenly, a flicker of grim hope gripped him. Running parallel with the track, and suspended from the roof by steel rods, was a bus-bar—a square-shaped pipe of alloy carrying live electric cables to the machines on the floor below.

Every few feet a length of cable flex was clipped by a three-point adapter into the bus-bar. These lengths of cable could be detached and moved farther along the bus-bar if required to service other machines.

Within hand's reach of Rod was an adapter, a cable attached to it.

So close was the travelling crane now that Rod's and Mat's outstretched bodies shook with the powerful throbbing of the five tons of machinery grinding towards them.

Rod ignored it. Forcing himself to icy calm, he shot out his hand and snatched the three-point adapter from its socket.

Mat saw him grip the three-core cable between his two hands and with desperate strength strive to tear it apart. It was tough, beyond the strength of most men to rip it in two; but with death now only inches away Rod's hands became like steel rippers—the cable snapped, dragging the insulation from its wires.

Rod's fingers worked furiously, twisting the wires together. His hand flashed out and he jammed the adapter back into its socket.

As he did so he felt the wheel of the crane brushing the hair which had tumbled forward over his perspiring brow.

Instantly, there was a flash; and from the floor below the loud hum of motors died to silence as the fused cable inside the bus-bar blew the power fuses.

The travelling crane stopped. Rod's pent-up breath rushed through his clenched teeth. Mat gulped and noticed with mounting excitement that the rising platform also had stopped. The electric motor had failed as had all the other electrically operated machines in the vast arms factory.

Rod's desperate action had brought the East Power's secret underground armaments works to a complete halt. Frantic shouts from the mystified workers below brought a brief grin to Mat's lips. But Rod ignored them. Over his shoulder he hissed a rapid instruction.

" Slither backwards, Mat, to the end of the track."

Mat backed quickly along the track, followed immediately by Rod. Thus they wormed their way along until they came to the end and Mat was forced to halt.

"Mat," Rod whispered. "There's an air duct behind you, and it's large enough to climb into."

Mat twisted his head. Rod was right. A circular tube resembling a ship's ventilator faced the end of the track. Through this, fresh air was blown into the underground arms factory. But with the power fuses burnt out, it was, through Rod's daring action, now lifeless.

Needing no telling, Mat thrust his feet across the short gap between the end of the track and the open mouth of the vent. His toes resting on the lip of the duct, he thrust his hands hard down and pushed his body backwards, letting his legs slither into the opening. With a final push he wriggled the rest of his body across the brief gap between the track and the duct and slid down inside it.

Rod kept careful watch on the floor below and on the men in the office on the gallery floor while Mat made his escape from the track.

Electricians were at work feverishly trying to replace the blown fuses. The East Power commander and his treacherous secret ally had rushed to the rail of the gallery to discover what had happened. The commander was almost dancing with fury, bellowing enraged orders for the electricians to get the machines working at once.

Suddenly the traitorous Chief of Staff looked up. Rod saw his glance fasten on the twisted cable hanging from its adapter alongside the track. Rod's heart sank when he saw the Chief of Staff point to the adapter.

The commander stared, then leaped back into his office, only to dash out a moment later with a pair of field-glasses which he focused on the broken cable. Then he let out a roar.

"Thunder," Rod groaned under his breath. "He's spotted what's happened!"

The commander's voice rose to a bellow as he pointed to the bus-bar and the gantry track alongside it. From the floor below a squad of soldiers rushed up the stairs of the gallery and along to the girder, shouldering their weapons, they leaped to the upright girders supporting the track above their heads.

"He's tumbled to the fact that we must

be hidden up here," Rod's thoughts raced. "And he's ordered them to climb the girders to hunt us on the travelling crane track."

The commander shouted an order to the two soldiers on the trolley platform stuck just below the level of the track.

The soldiers could not see over the track, but as the commander roared an order they raised their guns, and fired.

A thundering tattoo of murderous fire boomed beneath the roof of the vast underground factory. Rod's fists gripped tightly until his knuckles stood out like knots. He was being pinned down under a hail of bullets fanning to and fro above him, while the armed searchers were hurriedly scaling the girders in search of Mat and himself.

Unless he could follow Mat into the concealment of the air vent at the end of the track, he was as good as dead already. He had to reach the vent before the climbing soldiers reached the track and opened fire on him.

Rod made a lightning decision. If he attempted to follow Mat he was now certain to be seen; and not only he but Mat too would be killed.

At frantic speed, fearful of being seen if his body curved above the track's steel edge, he wormed forward towards the stationary travelling crane. He knew he was putting himself in danger of being crushed. If the electricians succeeded in repairing the fuses, the crane would at once resume its forward travel, and his plan would fail.

Reaching the huge iron wheels, Rod slid his hand down his leg and dragged up one leg of his trousers. Once more he searched in the polythene bag and this time brought out what looked like an ordinary pin.

Giving the head of the pin a sharp twist, he flicked it with his thumb and sent the pin whizzing over the edge of the track to the gallery below.

A loud, startling crack echoed up to him, followed by a bang—bang—bang—bang, like a series of rapid rifle shots.

He heard the East Power commander and the Tiban Chief of Staff yell out in startled alarm; then came the clatter of their boots as they dived for safety. A brief flicker of mirthless laughter creased Rod's lips. The pin's thunderous bangs were harmless, but they sounded exactly like a volley of fast shots.

The men climbing the girders ducked low, while the snipers on the platform switched their eyes to the gallery.

With a swift lift, Rod drew himself on to the crane and slid between its winding gear and electric motor housing. A coil of rope lay under the housing. He pulled it in front of him. He was now out of sight not only of anybody looking up from below, but also of the searchers on the upright girders.

Down on the floor, the startled electricians leaped back to their work of repairing the blown fuses, and the armed soldiers continued their hunting of the two white men. Suddenly, the travelling crane began to move again as the electricians completed their task.

Tensing himself, Rod travelled with the crane, watching carefully as it slowly came nearer and nearer to the end of the track. He peered cautiously from his concealment. The furious search was being concentrated up among the roof supports.

Finally, the crane reached the limit of its travel and ground to a halt. Rod edged stealthily from his hiding place, darting anxious glances over his shoulder as he thrust his body towards the mouth of the air vent. With a swift shove he hurtled across the brief space between the end of the track and the vent, and shot thankfully into the dark interior.

Slithering down inside the blackness, he thudded to his feet a short distance down. A glow of faint light came through a grill and he made out Mat at his side, eyeing him with grim anxiety.

"What happened?" Mat rapped in an anxious hiss.

Rod, ignoring the query, stared past his friend. Moving a little closer, he peered along the wide, circular ducting to the point where it ended in a grill at the other end. Light filtered through the air passage and the sound of voices could be heard faintly through the grill.

With Mat following, Rod crept cautiously and quietly along the duct to its far end. There he stopped and slowly put his face close to the grill. His eyes widened a little.

He was looking into the office of the commander, the same office where Mat had been held a prisoner! The East Power commander was alone except for the Chief of Staff of Barada's army who, a harsh smile on his face, was talking rapidly to the eager-faced commander.

"Barada will not dare countermand my orders to attack the British base at dawn," the Chief of Staff stated harshly and triumphantly. "He knows I hold his son prisoner and the boy will be put to death if Barada is fool enough to defy me."

"Very clever," the commander nodded, his eyes glittering with cruel satisfaction. "Where have you hidden Barada's small son?"

"Where Barada will never find him," came the snarling answer. "In a secret cave."

At this exchange, Rod clenched his teeth grimly. So the mystery as to why Barada, Britain's warm friend and ally, had suddenly ordered the British to quit the air base was, at last, explained. The treacherous Chief of Staff, in secret league with the East Power, had kidnapped Barada's small son, and by murderously threatening to slay the boy, he had forced the helpless Barada to do as he ordered!

Rod saw the East Power commander glance up at the clock.

"Come," he grated. "It is time to meet the Great One, our Leader!"

They strode from the office and Rod and Mat heard their boots marching down the steel steps of the gallery to the floor below.

Rod's fingers flashed to the grill, and with expert swiftness, quietly slipped off the spring clips holding it in place. Next instant he was pulling himself through the opening and jumping softly into the empty office. Mat followed.

Bent double, the two of them stole across the office to the window and, raising their heads to sill level, peered down at the vast steel floor below. What they saw brought gasps of amazement to their lips.

On roller bearings, the huge floor yawned open slowly and silently. Into view came the dark surface of water. The commander and his traitorous ally stood watching intently the gaping chasm, unaware of the interested spectators above them in the office.

Rod and Mat peering down in amazement from their vantage point, saw the dark waters stirring, then frothing, as from the depths there arose the conning tower and bridge of a long sinister submarine.

"By thunder!" Rod hissed. "This is not only a secret underground arms factory; it's also a secret submarine base. There must be an underwater channel from the sea."

Twisting his neck round, Rod flashed a glance at the clock. One hour to dawn! His eyes darted back to the submarine. On the bridge had appeared a figure in the uniform of the East Power. Unable to see the features clearly, Rod knew instinctively it was the man the commander had referred to as the Great One, the Leader! The East Power ruler!

The commander and the Chief of Staff came stiffly to attention, and behind them a guard of honour presented arms. The new arrival climbed down to the floor, now a make-shift quayside.

"He's come," Rod whispered, "to see the start of the operation against our air base. He hasn't long to wait," he added tensely, between tight lips.

Another uniformed figure had appeared on the bridge . . .

The Great One greeted the pair waiting on the quayside, and Rod and Mat saw him make a sign to the commander and Chief of Staff to move out of the hearing of the line of stiffly standing soldiers.

The three men disappeared under the gallery, out of sight of Rod and Mat. Rod dropped to his knees, crept out of the office and across the gallery, to peer cautiously over the rail in an effort to overhear the conversation below.

As Mat hopefully joined him, his glance fell on one of the girders rising to support the roof. Hoping to see what was going on without being detected from above or below, Mat crawled over to the girder and stood up slowly behind its shelter.

"Rod," he breathed, "they are studying a map. I can just see the edge of it, right beneath where I'm hidden by this girder."

Rod moved towards him, and Mat, in his eagerness, leaned forward over the rail. His foot pressed down on a patch of grease and, without warning, he slid head first over the rail.

Rod leaped forward but he was too late. Mat was falling through the air. Rod flashed to the rail, his heart pounding with fear for his friend crashing to sure death on the steel floor below.

A loud splash allayed his fears and Rod saw that Mat had hurtled into the dark depths of the water in which the submarine was now moored.

Mat vanished from sight. Rod held his breath until Mat's head bobbed to the surface. But the fall and the splash of Mat's body hitting the water had brought the guard of honour into action. As he spluttered in the water, a line of weapons covered him. Rod saw Mat hauled unceremoniously from the water—a prisoner of the East Power.

At top speed, Rod spun round and back to the office, dived through the grill and snapped it back into place. It was no use remaining on the gallery. That way he would be captured in moments and as a prisoner would be helpless to rescue Mat. The situation was desperate now—in less than an hour the army of Tiba, acting on the orders of its traitor chief, would launch a treacherous attack on the air base.

Rod squirmed back along the duct to the

foot of the open shaft leading up to the stationary crane. Pressing his hands and feet against the sides of the air passage, he battled his way up it to the open mouth near the roof. From there he eyed the grim scene on the floor below. Armed guards were grouped round the Great One, the commander and the Chief of Staff; facing them defiantly stood Mat. Rod saw the commander seize a microphone from one of his orderlies. Addressing the unseen Rod, the commander roared into the microphone.

"White spy, we have your partner. Unless you give yourself up within two minutes, your friend will be strapped to the bed of a drilling machine. A dozen drills will then bore through his body."

Rod listened with mounting horror and rage. Only by surrendering himself could Mat be saved from a terrible end!

Desperately, he sought for a means to rescue his co-agent. How could he outwit these ruthless, murderous people and save Mat?

Suddenly he stiffened and stared at the silent, stationary crane. Hanging down from the machine was a sturdy steel hook.

Rod slithered from the vent to the crane. Hidden from those below by the crane itself, he swiftly ran an expert eye over the tough, steel hook and the coil of rope under the electric motor housing.

The crane was almost at the end of its track. To accomplish the startling plan which had darted into his fertile brain, the crane must roll back along its travelling rail. The noise of its travel would be heard but that could not be helped. The success of his daring scheme must depend on its suddenness.

Slithering under the housing, Rod neatly and firmly ran a loop to one end of the rope coil and slid it over the steel hook of the crane. He hurriedly made a loop at the rope's other end, grasped it, then tripped the reversing switch.

The crane began its reverse travel. From the floor came startled shouts, but as he heard them Rod rose to his full height on the girdering at the end of the track. He put his foot in the end loop, and dived.

One foot free, gripping the rope with one hand only, he swung down and forward in a lightning curve, flashing feet first straight towards the group on the floor below. Before they realised what was happening Rod was exploding a path through them, his outstretched free foot smashing the commander to the floor, the looped foot sweeping the Great One on to his face as he flashed past the petrified Chief of Staff.

"Grab, Mat," he roared, his free hand stretched out. Mat, acting at lightning speed, threw himself towards Rod's flashing body and grabbed at the reaching hand.

The speed of Rod's flying body swept Mat off the floor and upwards over the heads of the guards, now tumbling into each other from the impact of Rod's feet. Weapons and men scattered to the floor.

Despite the combined weight of the two men the rope whizzed upward. Rod flicked a grim gaze at the travelling crane from which the rope hung. Split seconds counted. If the rope did not swing back fast enough, they could not make a flying landing on the girders at the far end! Mat and he would swing back to the floor below.

The rope reached the end of its upward surge. Rod threw his full strength into hurtling it down and back on its return swing. Right in their path of travel the scheming, evil Chief of Staff was jerking round, gun in hand, to face them.

"Get him, Mat," Rod thundered, and with a Herculean effort, he twisted the whistling rope so that they spun to one side of the howling mob struggling to its feet.

Mat's free hand flashed out. The Tiban Chief of Staff fired—Rod felt the bullet snip past him, then—Mat grabbed the traitor by his belt. Together, Rod gripping Mat, and Mat grasping the Chief of Staff like a sack, all three swung back and up—up to the girders.

"Let go, Mat," Rod roared as, with rising anxiety he realised that the crane had travelled too far for them to land feet first on the end girders. "Let go!"

Mat released his grip of the rope and, clutching his captive, hurtled through the air. With a body-shattering crash he landed on the girders, and Rod crashed at his side.

"Into the vent, Mat," Rod gasped. "I'll take care of this bird," and he reached down and snatched the gun from their prisoner's holster before the man knew what was happening.

Mat leaped at the vent and slid into it. Rod rammed the gun into his captive's ribs; his threatening expression and pointing finger made it clear to the terror-stricken Chief of Staff what he was to do.

Rod saw him cast a desperate look below as he stepped across the gap between the end of the track and the open mouth of the air duct. He was hoping for rescue. Rod shot a quick glance downwards.

One of the guards was staggering about pointing up at them. The East Power commander jerked his eyes upward and shouted a vengeful order. He felt no concern now for the Chief of Staff of the Tiban army; the traitor had already issued an order for his army to attack the British air base at dawn. So far as the East Power commander and his Leader, the Great One, were concerned, the Chief of Staff was no longer of value to them. He had done his treacherous work for them!

"Rapid fire," he screamed.

The East Power guards triggered their weapons. A blast of firing shattered the air in the enclosed factory and bullets zipped round Rod, now alone on the track—their prisoner had hurled himself into the duct a split second before the bullets screamed upward.

The steel track shielded Rod, but a deadly wall of hissing, whining lead formed an effective barrier between him and the mouth of the air vent.

Attracted by a movement, Rod turned to see guards scrambling up the girders. In a few moments they would be level with the track, and he would be an easy target for them.

Feverishly, he tugged off his shoes and slacks, rammed a trouser leg into each shoe, then tossed the bundle, shoes first, over the edge of the track.

From the floor below, the East Power guards saw what they thought was their human target tumbling from the track, and swung their rapid-fire weapons round to fire at Rod's desperate attempt at a decoy.

For a split second the enemy troops were fooled—their barrage of shots concentrated on the falling "figure." Rod leaped. Head-first he dived across the gap and threw himself into the mouth of the air duct.

He hurtled down inside the vent, his

hands thrust against the sides to brake his fall, his head bunched into his chest. As he slithered down the chute he heard, below, the sound of scuffling and hard breathing.

With a thud he landed on something soft. Gasping and groaning smote his ears as he staggered to his feet and peered at the man on whom he had fallen. Mat lay on the floor of the duct, dazed. Rod flashed a quick look along the duct to see their prisoner scrabbling frantically along on his hands and knees in a desperate bid to escape.

Rod jerked Mat to his feet.

"He fell on top of me," Mat gasped, dazedly. "Nearly knocked me out, then he tried to put a knife in me. Would have done, if you hadn't come sliding down. He made a bolt for it when he heard you coming."

"Come on," Rod gritted, breaking into a crawling chase along the low-roofed duct, his shoeless feet making no sound, the metal scraping his bare knees. "We've got to recapture him before he can get away. It's our only chance to stop the attack on our base in less than an hour."

The shadowy figure ahead was suddenly silhouetted against a filter panel. Rod could see him tearing at the panel's clips, so that he could drag it away and hurl himself from the duct.

Rod forgot his sore, bare knees and threw himself after his quarry. The traitor had succeeded in tearing away the panel and was half-way through it, bellowing for help at the top of his voice.

Rod and Mat heard answering yells, followed by the thud of pounding feet. If the rescuers arrived too soon and succeeded in hauling the Chief of Staff free, Rod knew it would be the end for him and Mat. Trapped in the duct they would be fired at through the open panel and shot down like rats in a hole.

Rod dug his stockinged feet into the flooring and threw himself in a headlong dive along the duct. His outstretched hands grabbed the legs of the escaper, and, with a furious tug, he pulled him back into the duct.

His bunched fist crashed into the other's jaw and the traitor sagged back, unconscious. Ruthlessly, Rod slung the inert man over his back and surged on and past the open panel, Mat hard on his heels.

"Keep going, Mat," he panted over his shoulder. "This vent is sucking in fresh air, so it must lead to the outside world."

Echoing along the shaft, they could hear their pursuers clambering through the open panel after them. With his burden still on his back, Rod dug into the polythene bag strapped to his bare leg, and, fishing out the smoke pellet, tossed it back to Mat. Immediately, Mat triggered it and hurled it behind him.

"That'll drive 'em back," Rod gasped. "The smoke will choke 'em if they try to crawl through it."

Another filter came in sight. Just as he was about to crawl hurriedly past, Rod darted a glance through the opening. Mat saw him halt suddenly and again reach into the bag on his shin, before ripping away the filter panel.

"It's the bomb store, the other side of this air filter," Rod rapped in a tense voice. "I'm going to drop a time-charge through the panel. Here goes."

Swiftly, Rod spun a tiny numbered gauge on a micro-sized explosive charge, then he lobbed it through the vent opening. The charge rolled and came to rest under a rack of mortar bombs. As Mat passed the filter panel he took a quick peep into the store and saw that it was packed with rockets, mortar bombs and grenades.

"Hurry, Mat," Rod panted. "I've given the charge five minutes."

With his unconscious burden on his back and Mat in the rear, Rod crawled at a furious pace along the duct, scraped knees and shins forgotten. The duct echoed with the yells and thunderous shouts of the East Power soldiers and their commander, who were held back by the choking clouds of smoke.

Rod, his head low, crashed head-first into something solid. He shook himself and raised his eyes. Mat heard him utter a gasp of triumph.

"It's the grill over the mouth of the air vent," Rod croaked. "I can see the stars. We've made it, Mat!"

Fingers crooked round the metal bars, Rod gripped the grill to tear it free. But it stayed firm. Behind him, Mat heard Rod's hiss of dismay and saw him flash a glance at his illuminated watch. Three minutes—and the time-charge was due to explode! The grill was screwed firmly in place, and in thirty minutes it would be dawn!

From his shin-bag, Rod whipped out what looked like a pencil torch. A quick twist on the base of the apparatus and a flame hissed out. Rod played it on to the first of the screw heads.

"It's an efficient enough flame cutter," Rod gritted through his teeth, "But we've barely time for it to cut through the screws."

The first of the screw heads hissed to the floor. Steadily, while Mat watched breathlessly, Rod went to work on the second screw, then the third. With a clatter the last fell away and, ignoring the searing heat of the metal grill, Rod grabbed it with both hands and tore it free.

He thrust his captive out of the aperture and dived after him. Mat followed like a bolting rabbit. Rod shouldered his unconscious prisoner and side by side he and

Mat ran down the hill covering the secret underground arms factory.

At the foot of the hill, Rod slid to a halt at the edge of a pool of water and plunged the traitor's head in and out of the water. The shock jerked the Chief of Staff back to consciousness. He spluttered and sat up.

"Listen," Rod hissed through clenched teeth. "You are going to radio your ruler, Barada, to order his troops to return to their barracks at once. They will not launch the treacherous attack on the British air base at dawn!"

The traitor's eyes narrowed to slits.

"Never," he snarled. "And you dare do nothing. I have the Barada's small son prisoner. The Barada dare not defy me; he has my orders, and he will carry them out."

Rod's jaw tightened. The traitor spoke the truth. The Barada would not halt the attack for fear of what would happen to his son! And only the Barada's command could prevent the Tiban army attacking at dawn, twenty-eight minutes hence!

Over his shoulder Rod snapped an order to Mat.

"Cut down a length of liana vine," he gritted. "We're going to bind him, hand and foot. The vine is strong and tough; he'll never break it."

It was done in seconds. The manacled traitor lay on the ground at the foot of the hill, glaring up at Rod and Mat, a sneer on his curled lips.

"I have beaten you," he jeered. "Barada would not obey you, even if you threatened to assassinate him. He knows that to defy me would mean his small son's death. And only I know where the boy is hidden."

Rod spun round to Mat, making it seem as if he had no further use for the traitor. Rapidly he spoke a warning.

"Come on, we've got to get clear. This traitor is going to stay where he is. In two minutes the arms factory under the hill will blow sky high. And he will go up with it," he added in a grim voice.

Both men turned as though to race to safety.

The traitorous Chief of Staff let out a howl of terror. Rod's words and tone convinced him the white man was not bluffing. He screamed in fear.

"Stop! Stop! I will do as you say."

In a flash Rod was slashing him free, then he thrust his micro-transmitter in the man's face.

"Call Barada and tell him where his son is hidden," he thundered in a voice full of urgency. "And tell him to order his troops back to their barracks."

His voice quaking, the traitor obeyed. Rod and Mat thrilled with triumph as they heard Barada answering, his voice trembling with joy. Seconds later, Rod and Mat heard through their receiver the Barada commanding his army to march back immediately to their barracks.

"Quick," Rod snapped. "Run Mat; and you too, traitor. We're handing you over to Barada, your ruler. Run for your lives."

At breakneck speed they ran deep into the jungle, away from the hill.

Behind them they heard a low rumble, then a thunderous roar which went on and on as, below the hill, the secret underground arms factory of the East Power exploded into a heaving, flying mass of concrete and torn steel.

Rod and Mat turned and looked back.

Dawn was breaking and in its faint light they saw an immense cloud of dust rising. They eyed it grimly.

"That's the end of the East Power's sinister schemes," Rod said with quiet triumph. "And now the Barada will, once more, be a faithful and warm ally of Britain."

And with their prisoner gripped between them, the triumphant British security agents hurried on their way to meet the Barada.